To Lily

For everything there is a season

The LonelyTree

NICHOLAS HALLIDAY

The Lonely Tree has a new friend called ....
Write your name here

For fun and games and to discover more about the animals hiding in the pages
of this book visit the website at **www.thelonelytree.co.uk**

It was spring in the New Forest.

A carpet of bluebells crept over the forest floor. On the branches above, new leaves had turned the canopy into a blanket of emerald jewels.

As the days grew warmer, the birds who had flown to Africa in the autumn were returning from their winter holidays.

Late one rainy night, something beneath the leaves began to move, sending ripples out through the shallow puddles.

The next morning the forest woke to an unusual sight.

At the foot of the oldest oak a new tree had begun to grow.
No one but the oldest oak had seen anything like it before.

"It certainly isn't like any of us," said the others.

It was summer in the New Forest.

The oak greeted the little tree.
"Welcome to the New Forest," he said.
"This is your home and we are your friends."

The little tree grew quickly and
before long the old oak began telling
stories of life in the forest.

Oak trees can fill a whole summer with stories, but the oldest oak told the best stories of all. Born long ago, he could remember a time when the New Forest really was new, and dragons still roamed the earth.

All through the summer the little tree listened in wonder, and grew taller and stronger every day.

He and the old oak became the best of friends.

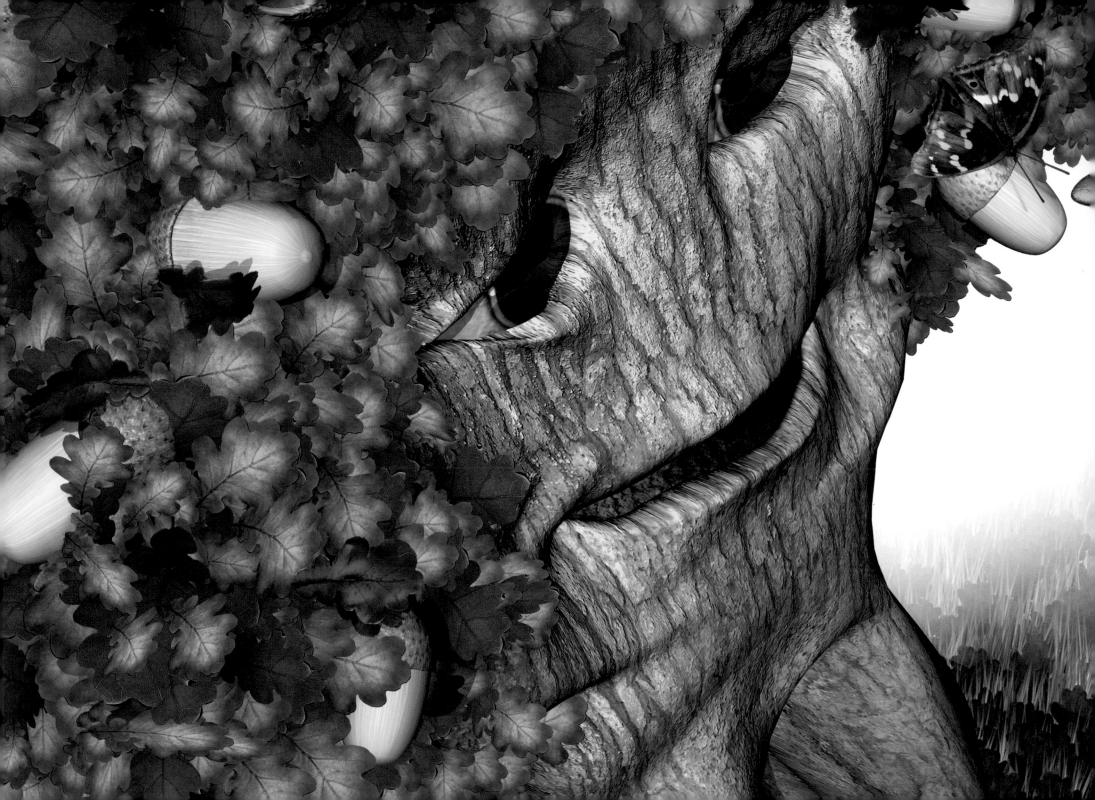

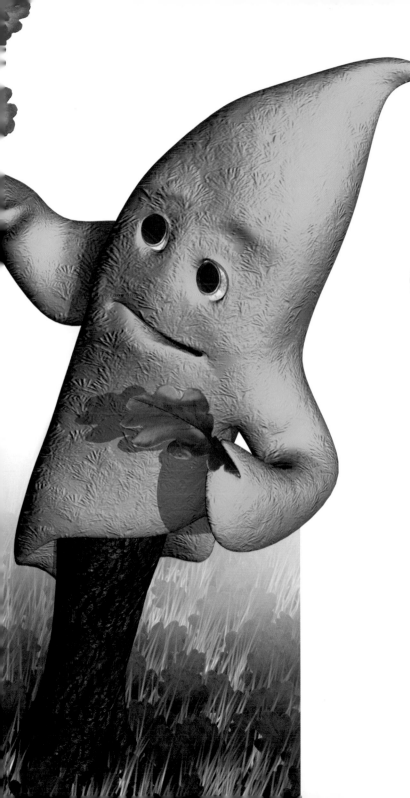

It was autumn in the New Forest.

One afternoon after listening to a particularly
beautiful story, the little tree noticed something.

"Some of your leaves have turned brown,"
he said to his old friend.
"This happens to all oak trees," his friend replied.
"I am preparing to go to sleep for the winter."
"Will I sleep too?" asked the little tree.
"No," the old oak answered. "You are evergreen,
and evergreens never sleep."

Acorns fell with the leaves and covered the ground in deep seasonal colour.

On the last damp evening of autumn,
the birds flew away to the warmth of Africa,
and the last acorn fell from the old oak.

"I am very tired," he said to his little friend,
"I have to sleep now. Always remember that I love you."

It was winter in the New Forest.

The little tree became very cold ...

... and very lonely.

Sheets of white snow covered the forest.

The only winter visitor was a graceful barn owl who
perched on top of the old oak on Christmas morning.

"There are bright coloured lights in the town," he called,
"and children are singing carols in the churchyard."

As the owl flew away the lonely tree
felt lonelier than ever.

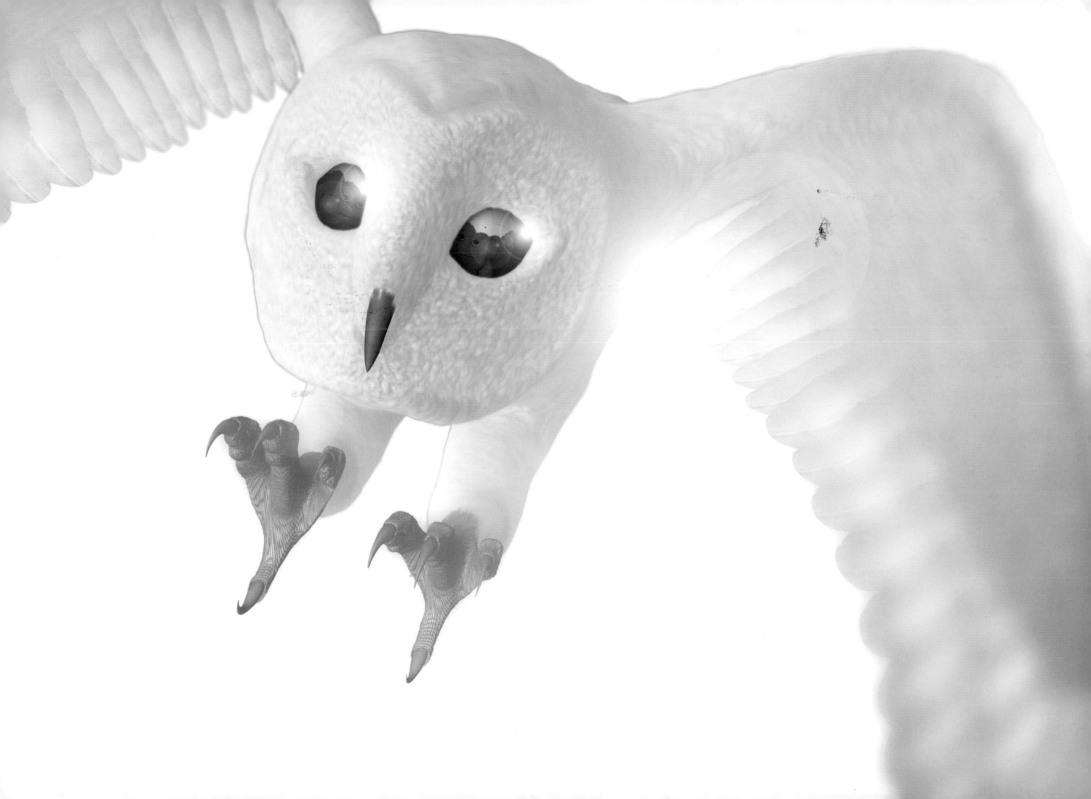

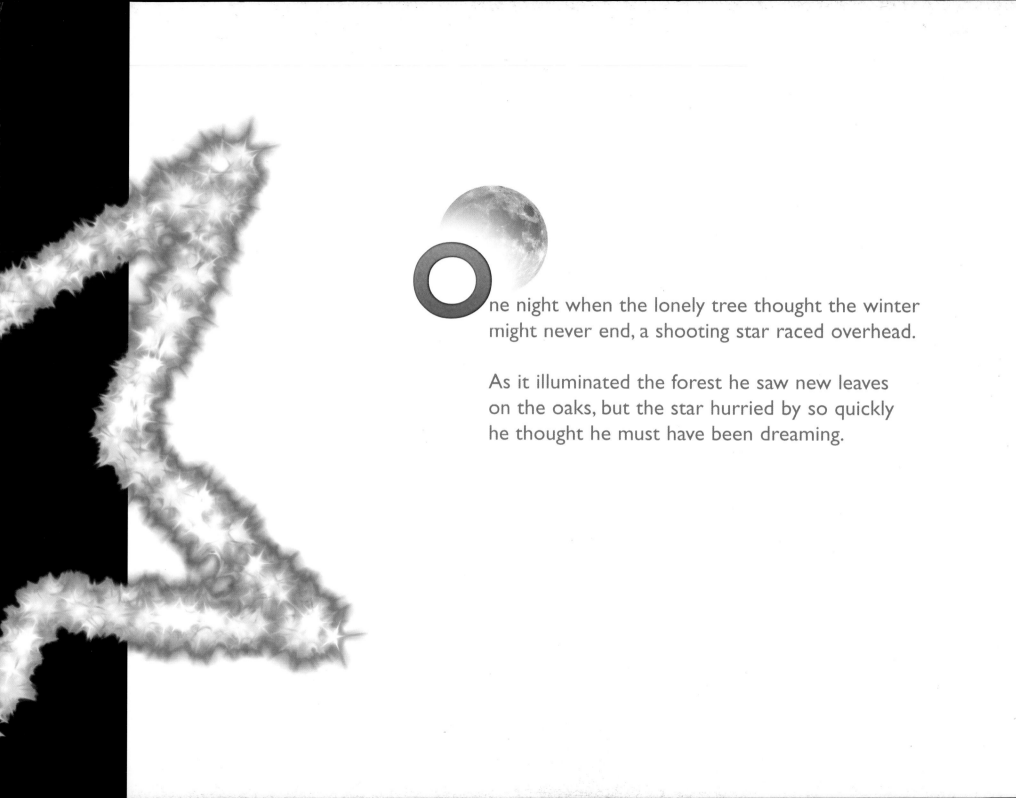

One night when the lonely tree thought the winter might never end, a shooting star raced overhead.

As it illuminated the forest he saw new leaves on the oaks, but the star hurried by so quickly he thought he must have been dreaming.

It was spring in the New Forest.

Next morning a wonderful sight greeted the lonely tree.

A carpet of bluebells crept over the forest floor.
On the branches above, new leaves had again turned
the canopy into a blanket of emerald jewels.

But something was wrong. There was not a single
new leaf on the branches of his old friend.

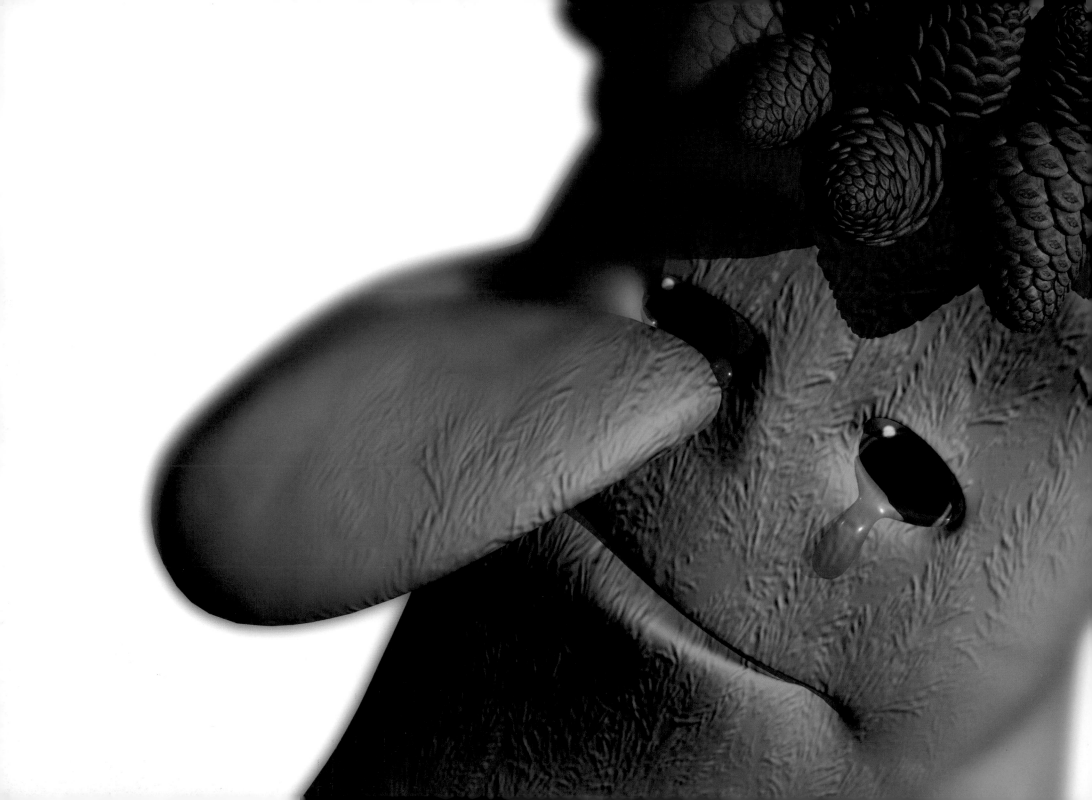

Days passed, and once again the birds
returned to the forest.

"Why is my friend still asleep?" asked the lonely tree.
"His long life has ended," replied the other
oaks with sadness. "He has died."

The lonely tree did not understand.

"Death is a part of life," they told him.
"He will never wake up, but his love will
be with us forever."

T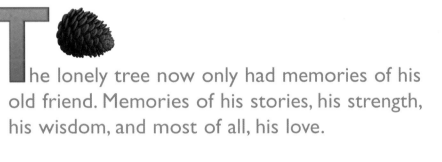he lonely tree now only had memories of his old friend. Memories of his stories, his strength, his wisdom, and most of all, his love.

One late spring day when the lonely tree was feeling especially sad, a miraculous thing happened.

In the very place where that last acorn had fallen, a tiny oak tree was beginning to grow.

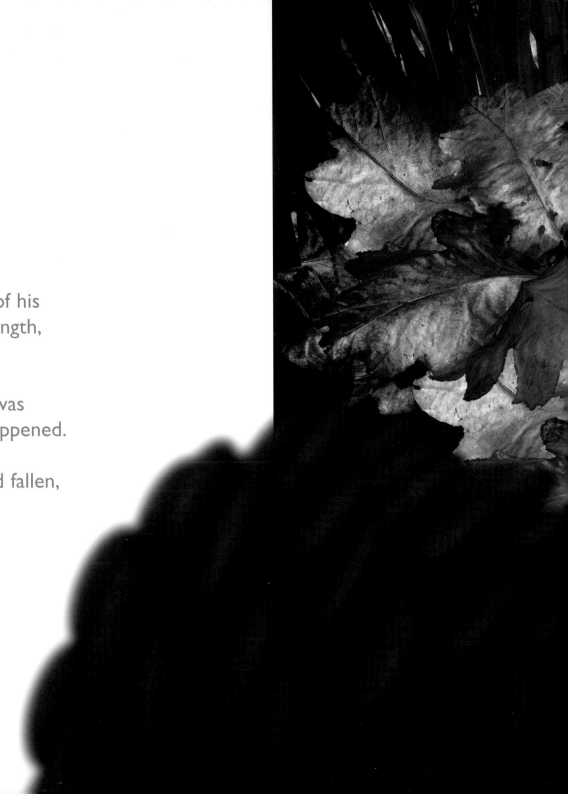

It was summer in the New Forest.

It was the first of many wonderful summers.

The lonely tree greeted the little oak and
began retelling stories of life in the forest.

As they grew, their roots went deeper
and deeper into the ground.

Now the lonely tree understood that
for everything there was a season.

Summer brings warmth and the time to grow.
Autumn provides us with seeds for the future.
Without a friend, winter can be cold and lonely,
but spring always brings new life.

The two trees can still be seen in the New Forest,
and they are of course, the best of friends.

Nicholas with daughter Lily

ABOUT THE AUTHOR

NICHOLAS HALLIDAY studied at Epsom School of Art and Design, Lancashire University and Kingston University. Since graduating from Kingston in 1991 with a BA in graphic design, he has worked as an author, illustrator and designer and now runs the independent children's publisher HallidayBooks. He has a daughter Lily, to whom *The Lonely Tree* is dedicated.

ACKNOWLEDGMENTS

My sincere thanks go to Paul Shenton for his friendship and unconditional support. Without his help this book would never have been published.

Thanks also go to Simon Flynn and Andrew Furlow at Icon Books for their invaluable advice. I would also like to thank my mother Jennifer, for her constant encouragement.

Finally, my love and thanks go to my beautiful daughter Lily, for inspiring me and for simply being herself.

HALLIDAYBOOKS
www.hallidaybooks.com

Written and illustrated by NICHOLAS HALLIDAY

This edition published 2012 · First published 2006 · ISBN: 978-0-9539459-8-6

www.hallidaybooks.com · www.thelonelytree.co.uk

2006 © Nicholas Halliday and HallidayBooks

The author has asserted his moral rights · All rights reserved

No part of this publication may be reproduced in any way without prior permission in writing from the publisher

Printed and bound by Hong Kong Graphics & Printing Ltd